Maxine Zohn Bozzo
PICTURES BY Frank Modell

TOBY IN THE COUNTRY, TOBY IN THE CITY

Greenwillow Books, New York

TO JAY MACHLIS, WHO WILL LIVE IN OUR HEARTS FOREVER

Text copyright © 1982
by Maxine Zohn Bozzo
Illustrations copyright ©
1982 by Frank Modell
All rights reserved. No part
of this book may be reproduced
without permission from
Greenwillow Books, a division
of William Morrow & Company, Inc.
105 Madison Ave., N.Y., N.Y. 10016.
Printed in U.S.A. First Edition
5 4 3 2 1
Library of Congress
Cataloging in Publication Data
Bozzo, Maxine Zohn.
Toby in the country, Toby in the city.
Summary: Although one Toby lives in the city and
the other in the country, and one is a boy and the
other a girl, they both enjoy similar things.
[1. City and town life—Fiction.   2. Country life—
Fiction] I. Modell, Frank, ill. II. Title.
PZ7.B6975To   [E]   81-7274
ISBN 0-688-00916-6   AACR2
ISBN 0-688-00917-4 (lib. bdg.)

I live in the country, and my name is Toby.

I live in the city, and my name is Toby.

My house looks like this.

My house looks like this.

My street looks like this, and has trees.

My street looks like this, and has trees.

I go to school with my sister and brother.

I go to school with my sister and brother.

After school I like to play with my friends.

After school I like to play with my friends.

Sometimes it's winter in the country...
and I like to play in the snow.

Sometimes it's winter in the city...
and I like to play in the snow.

When it is spring in the country...
I see lots of flowers.

When it is spring in the city...
I see lots of flowers.

When summer comes to the country...
I like to go to the beach.

When summer comes to the city...
I like to go to the beach.

Sometimes when it is fall in the country...
I like to play in the leaves.

Sometimes when it is fall in the city...
I like to play in the leaves.

I like to live in the country.

I like to live in the city.

I like to visit the city.

I like to visit the country.

And I LIKE YOU!

DATE DUE